Here is a tale of enchantment, a fairy-tale with a twist, drawn from those old times "when it was still of some use to wish for the things one wanted." This is the story of a beautiful King's daughter, who one day lost a favorite plaything, and of an ugly frog who held her to a promise she didn't want to keep. Although it is not as famous as some other tales the Grimm Brothers faithfully recorded, THE FROG PRINCE has been a favorite of generations of children and romantics, including Paul Galdone. His long-time wish has been to present his own edition for the readers whose favorite he is.

THE FROG PRINCE

THE FROG

Adapted from the retelling by the Brothers Grimm

PRINCE

by Paul Galdone

McGRAW-HILL BOOK COMPANY

New York   St. Louis   San Francisco   Düsseldorf   Johannesburg   Kuala Lumpur   London
Mexico   Montreal   New Delhi   Panama   Rio de Janeiro   Singapore   Sydney   Toronto

For Eleanor

Library of Congress Cataloging in Publication Data appears on last page

THE FROG PRINCE is an adaptation of the story which appeared in
HOUSEHOLD STORIES by the Brothers Grimm, translated by Lucy
Crane, and first published by Macmillan and Company in 1886.

123456789 RABP 7898765

In the old times, when it was still of some use to wish for the thing one wanted, there lived a King whose daughters were all handsome, but the youngest was so beautiful that the sun himself, who had seen so much, wondered each time he shone over her because of her beauty.

Near the royal castle there was a great dark wood, and in the wood under an old linden tree was a well. When the day was hot, the King's daughter used to go forth into the wood and sit by the brink of the cool well. And if the time seemed long, she would take out a golden ball and throw it up and catch it again, for this was her favorite pastime.

Now it happened one day that the golden ball, instead of falling back into the maiden's little hand which had sent it aloft, dropped to the ground near the edge of the well and rolled in. The King's daughter followed it with her eyes as it sank, but the well was deep, so deep that the bottom could not be seen. Then she began to weep, and she wept and wept as if she could never be comforted.

And in the midst of her weeping she heard a voice saying to her,

"What ails thee, King's daughter? Your tears would melt a heart of stone."

And when she looked to see where the voice came from, there was nothing but a frog stretching his thick ugly head out of the water.

"Oh, it is you, old waddler?" said she. "I weep because my golden ball has fallen into the well."

"Never mind, do not weep," answered the frog. "I can help you. But what will you give me if I fetch up your ball again?"

"Whatever you like, dear frog," said she. "Any of my clothes, my pearls, or even the golden crown that I wear."

"Your clothes, your pearls and jewels, and your golden crown are not for me," answered the frog. "But if you would love me, and have me for your companion and playfellow, and let me sit by you at table and eat from your plate and drink from your cup, and sleep in your little bed—if you would promise all this, then I would dive below the water and fetch your golden ball again for you."

"Oh yes," she answered. "I will promise it all, whatever you want, if only you will get me my ball again."

But, she thought to herself, "What nonsense he talks! As if he could do anything but sit in the water and croak with the other frogs, or could possibly be anyone's companion."

But the frog, as soon as he heard her promise, drew his head under the water and sank out of sight. After a while he came to the surface again with the ball in his mouth, and threw it on the grass.

The King's daughter was overjoyed to see her pretty plaything again, and she caught it up and ran off with it.

"Stop, stop!" cried the frog. "Take me up too. I cannot run as fast as you!"

But it was of no use, for croak, croak after her as he might, she would not listen to him. Instead, she made haste home and very soon forgot all about the poor frog, who had to betake himself to his well again.

The next day, when the King's daughter was
sitting at the table with the King and all the
court, and was eating from her golden plate, there
came the sound of something pitter patter hop-hop-hopping
and stepping up the marble stairs,
and there came a knocking at the door, and a voice
crying, "Youngest King's daughter, let me in!"

She got up to see who it could be, but
when she opened the door, there was the frog
sitting outside. Then she shut the door hastily
and went back to her seat, feeling very uneasy.

The King noticed how quickly her heart was beating
and said,

"My child, what are you afraid of? Is there a
giant standing at the door ready to carry you away?"

"Oh no," answered she. "No giant, but a horrid frog."

"And what does the frog want?" asked the king.

"Oh, dear father," answered she. "When I was sitting by the well yesterday playing with my golden ball, it fell into the water. And while I was crying for the loss of it, the frog came and got it again for me on condition I would let him be my companion. I never thought that he could leave the water and come after me; but now there he is outside the door and he wants to come in to me."

Then they all heard him knocking the second
time and crying:

> "Youngest King's daughter,
> Open to me!
> By the well water
> What promised you me?
> Youngest King's daughter
> Now open to me!"

"That which you have promised must you perform,"
said the King. "So now go and let him in."
So she went and opened the door and the frog
hopped in, following at her heels till she reached
her chair.

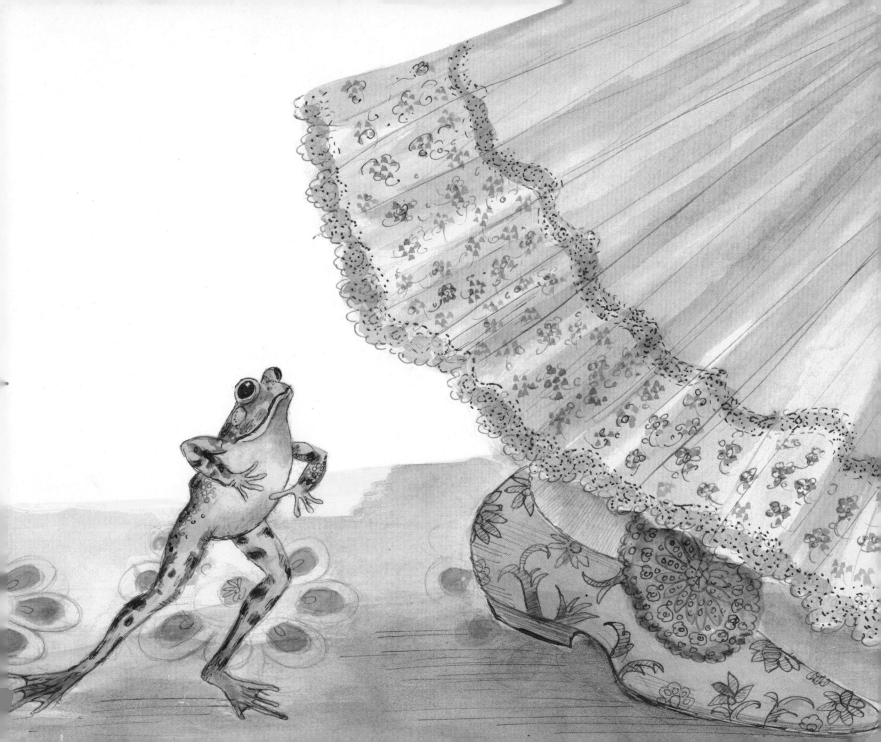

Then he stopped and cried, "Lift me up to sit by you."

But she delayed doing so until the King ordered her. When once the frog was on the chair, he wanted to get on the table, and there he sat and said,

"Now push your golden plate a little nearer so that we may eat together."

And so she did, but everybody could see how unwilling she was. The frog feasted heartily, but every morsel seemed to stick in her throat.

"I have had enough now," said the frog at last.

"And as I am tired you must carry me to your room and make ready your silken bed, and we will lie down and go to sleep."

Then the King's daughter began to weep for she was afraid of the cold frog, whom nothing would satisfy but he must sleep in her pretty clean bed.

Now the King grew angry with her and said,

"That which you have promised in your time of necessity, you must now perform."

So she picked up the frog with her finger and
thumb, carried him upstairs, and put him in a corner.

When she had lain down to sleep, he came hopping up, saying, "I am tired and want to sleep as much as you. Take me up, or I will tell your father."

Then she felt beside herself with rage, and
picking him up, she threw him with all her strength
against the wall, crying,
   "Now will you be quiet, you horrid frog!"

But as he fell he ceased to be a frog, and
became all at once a prince with beautiful kind eyes.

And so it came to pass that with her father's consent they became bride and bridegroom. And he told her how a wicked witch had bound him by her spells, and how no one but she alone could have released him, and that they two would go together to his father's kingdom.

And there came to the door a carriage drawn by eight white horses, with red plumes on their heads and with golden harness, and behind the carriage was standing faithful Henry, the servant of the young prince.

Now, faithful Henry had suffered such care and pain when his master was turned into a frog that he had been obliged to wear three iron bands over his heart, to keep it from breaking with trouble and anxiety.

When the carriage was to take the prince
to his kingdom, and faithful Henry had helped them
both in, he got up behind and was full of joy at
his master's deliverance.

And when they had gone a part of the way, the
prince heard a sound at the back of the carriage
as if something had broken, and he turned around
and cried,
   "Henry, the wheel must be breaking!"
But Henry answered,

> "The wheel does not break,
>   'Tis the band round my heart
>   That to lessen its ache,
>   When I grieved for your sake,
>   I bound round my heart."

Again and yet once again there was the same sound,
and the prince thought it must be a wheel breaking,
but it was the breaking of the other bands from
faithful Henry's heart, because it was now so relieved
and happy.

Library of Congress Cataloging in Publication Data

Main entry under title:

The Frog prince.

   SUMMARY: As payment for retrieving the princess'
ball, the frog exacts a promise which the princess is
reluctant to fulfill.
   [1. Fairy tales. 2. Folklore—Germany] I. Grimm,
Jakob Ludwig Karl, 1785-1863. Der Froschkönig.
II. Galdone, Paul, illus.
PZ8.F9149   398.2'1'0943 [E]   73-17447
ISBN 0-07-022688-1
ISBN 0-07-022689-X (lib. bdg.)

Paul Galdone drew the Frog Prince from life. His models were caught in a pond on his Vermont farm. They reluctantly posed for short spells and were returned to the pond by the grateful artist before they grew too tired.